Aunt CeeCee, Aunt Belle, and Mama's Surprise

Mary Quattlebaum

Illustrated by Michael Chesworth

A Doubleday Book for Young Readers

A Doubleday Book for Young Readers
Published by
Random House, Inc.
1540 Broadway
New York, New York 10036
Doubleday and the portrayal of an anchor with a dolphin are trademarks of
Random House, Inc.
Text copyright © 1999 by Mary Quattlebaum
Illustrations copyright © 1999 by Michael Chesworth

Library of Congress Cataloging-in-Publication Data
Quattlebaum, Mary.
    Aunt CeeCee, Aunt Belle, and Mama's surprise / Mary Quattlebaum; illustrated by Michael
Chesworth.
        p.   cm.
    Summary: Because nitpicking Aunt Belle and slapdash Aunt CeeCee help plan the surprise
party for her mother's birthday, the young planner faces lots of frenzy and confusion.
    ISBN 0-385-32275-5
    [1. Aunts—Fiction.   2. Birthdays—Fiction.   3. Parties—Fiction.]
I. Chesworth, Michael, ill.   II. Title.
PZ7Q19Au   1999
[E]—dc21

                                                                        97-40357
                                                                            CIP
                                                                            AC

jj FDL

The text of this book is set in 20-point Powhatten.
Book design by Trish Parcell Watts
Manufactured in the United States of America
June 1999
10 9 8 7 6 5 4 3 2 1

To Jean, Mary, Jillian, and Elyse,
four wonderful, take-charge girls
—M.Q.

The illustrations in this book
were inspired by and are an homage to
the work of John Held, Jr.,
illustrator of the Jazz Age.
—M.C.

Aunt CeeCee Mama Me Aunt Belle

Daddy

THE PLAYERS

Those Cats

Sarah & Squeal J.P. Jolene Flo

Mama loves to drink tea and chat with her sisters. Aunt CeeCee is youngest, Aunt Belle is oldest, and Mama is plunk in the middle. They are forever trading clothes, visits, secrets, dishes. And you should hear them swap stories! The same long-ago tales get told in three different ways.

But I figured I'd better take charge of telling this story, the Story of Mama's Surprise.

My aunts . . . well, they don't tell this story quite right.

It was just last year and Mama's birthday was coming. She said she did not want a big birthday fuss. No presents, no party, no cake.

She said that at least once a day.

I knew better. Mama loves a birthday—anyone's birthday—and the fuss that comes once a year.

So while Mama rattled teacups in the kitchen, I pulled her sisters—my aunts—aside . . .

And we whispered about a surprise.

We made a "to invite" list
of family and friends.

We made a "to buy" list
of streamers and hats.

We made three "to do" lists to
divide the tasks among
Aunt CeeCee, Aunt Belle, and me.

We set a date (June 6, the day Mama was born),
a time (six o'clock), and a place
(Aunt Belle's home).

Our surprise-party plans were brilliant. Mama would never suspect.

Of course, we did not make a list of possible problems.

What could ever go wrong?

Let me tell you, plenty went wrong.

Aunt CeeCee's girl Flo boo-hooed and sulked unless she was part of each plan—and then mixed every plan up. The little ones had to be constantly watched. Sarah could not keep the tiniest secret. Squeal shouted out all the wrong words.

And Aunt Belle's pride and joy, her baby boy, who is tall as a tree— well, J.P. tied up the phone both morning and night yakking with his girlfriend Jolene.

Not to mention the cats! The family of cats.

The big, BIG family
of cats.

No bag, box, or bow
was safe from those cats.

Their whiskers were
in everything.

Daddy could not remember
the password.

Aunt CeeCee slapdashed
at the very last minute.

Aunt Belle nitpicked
the tiniest things.

But Mama's June 6 surprise day finally came.
I had the perfect present, wrapped up so nicely and tied with a bow.
Daddy dropped me off at Aunt Belle's house.

I'll call when the party is ready. Don't forget to bring Mama.

What's that password again? Broccoli and Butter? Macaroni and Cheese?

Daddy! Broccoli and Cheese!

And *I* got a BIG surprise.

Aunt CeeCee's cake was still as bald as a stone and the frosting half made in a bowl.

Aunt Belle fretted over her tape.

Flo read from some list, Sarah turned cartwheels, Squeal lived up to his name.

And J.P.—well, I couldn't spy his six-foot-tall self . . .

. . . but I heard his yak-yakking voice.

As for those cats! That family of cats. That big, BIG family of cats . . .

They were playing Tarzan with the streamers and hippo with the punch.

The clock tick-ticked toward six.

It is a good thing—a very good thing—that I'm a take-charge kind of girl.

At 5:45 the doorbell rang.
As folks arrived with their presents, pie tins, grins, and good wishes, they took one look at that birthday room . . .
And everyone pitched in and helped.

Oh, Jolene!

Candles!
Tape!
Balloons!
Hats!

Oh, J.P.!

J.P., pleeeze get OFF that phone!

When I finally could call home to talk to my daddy, to say, "The party is ready, bring the birthday girl NOW"—guess who answered the phone?

We turned out the lights and hid where we could.

And when the door squeaked open and
I saw Mama's shoe, I was the first to yell.

I will never forget the look on her face.

Oh, Mama loved the fuss! She loved the bows, bags, cat games, and chips. She loved the streamers, punch, cartwheels, and squeals.

There was singing and dancing. The cake was gobbled and declared delicious. Aunt Belle put on the kettle for tea.

Then Mama unwrapped my present.

This surprise-party story is now a favorite with Mama and her sisters. Over tea, visiting one home or the other, as the "I remembers" get passed back and forth, sooner or later they will trot out this tale.

But somehow, my aunts get confused in the telling. Aunt Belle says her nitpicking saved the party. Aunt CeeCee swears it was her slapdash, last-minute style.

Mama knows better. She takes a big hot-tea swallow from her birthday cup.

She knows I'm a take-charge kind of girl, good at doing what needs to be done.

And when I tell my side of the story, she smiles.

Well, then I yelled, "Candles, tape, balloons, hats!" Aunt Belle, Aunt Cee Cee, and Flo said, "Help!" and Squeal squealed. J.P. was yakking on the phone. Then the doorbell rang. The room was a mess! The clock was tick-ticking to six. And then...

The End